Sam took the feather
and turned to the table.

The lady blazed up in golden light. Her armor and helmet reflected the sun. The huge white owl on her shoulder looked at Sam. Its eyes were as round as a full moon. The round eyes blinked. The owl nodded its head.

Sam nodded back.

Then the golden light and the owl were gone.

Joe was holding the feather again. "I think she's Athena," he said. "The goddess of wisdom."

Wind Spell

THE THIRD BOOK IN

The Magic Elements Quartet

by Mallory Loehr

A Stepping Stone Book™

RANDOM HOUSE NEW YORK

Published in the United States by Random House, Inc., New York, and
simultaneously in Canada by Random House of Canada Limited, Toronto.

www.randomhouse.com/kids

Library of Congress Catalog Card Number: 00-38716
ISBN: 0-679-89217-6

Printed in the United States of America June 2000 10 9 8 7 6 5 4 3 2 1

Random House, Inc. New York, Toronto, London, Sydney, Auckland

For my brother Aidan
and in memory of my Uncle Ned

Contents

Prologue

First it refused to carry his thunderbolts. Then it folded its wings and wouldn't fly.

He called one of his daughters and asked her advice. His daughter listened to the problem and nodded wisely. Then she asked her father to send her three feathers from the lonely animal's wings.

Far away in another time, an old blind man felt the wind change.

CHAPTER ONE

Feathers

Something was falling from the sky. Sam squinted up into the mist and tried to see it better. Was it a bird? Or had someone dropped something from a balloon? Whatever it was, the wind nudged it over so that it headed right toward him.

Sam shouted to his older brother and sister. Joe and Polly joined Sam on the patch of dewy grass at the top of the mountain.

Sam pointed up.

The falling thing became three falling

things, then three white feathers. But the feathers weren't drifting softly, as feathers should. They fell like arrows, slicing through the swirling clouds.

"Catch," whispered the wind.

Sam, Polly, and Joe raised their arms. Each caught a feather in uplifted hands.

Polly brought her hands down. The feather was almost as long as her arm. She ran a finger along one soft edge. Colors shimmered through it like a soap bubble. She couldn't help smiling.

Sam held his feather tightly. He could feel how strong it was as it pushed against the wind. He smiled, too.

Sam and Polly looked at each other, then turned to their older brother.

Joe was examining his feather. He looked very serious. "What kind of bird do you think it's from?" he asked.

"A *magic* bird," answered Polly.

Sam nodded his agreement.

"Don't be silly," scoffed Joe.

"But didn't you see how they fell?" asked Polly. "That was *not* normal. And one feather came to each of us. Like it was meant to be."

"Yeah," said Sam. "And soon we'll get a note or a message about what we're supposed to do. *I* think we'll get to fly!"

"They're cool feathers," said Joe. "But they are *not* magic."

"What's the matter with you?" asked Polly, sounding like their mother on a bad day. "Don't tell me you don't remember the bottle with the wishes?"

"That was just a game we played," Joe said, smiling condescendingly.

"And what about the voice?" asked Polly. "Didn't you hear it?"

"It said 'catch,'" said Sam.

Joe looked uncomfortable. "That was just the wind...," he said.

Polly rolled her eyes. "Fine. Be that way. *We're* going to find the directions." She looked over at Sam. "Right?"

Sam nodded and gave Joe an apologetic glance. "We told you about the earth magic," he said. "It really happened. And the water wishes...you *have* to remember."

Joe held up his feather. He frowned as he tried to make up his mind. He thought about the beach the summer before. It seemed like a strange dream. And the story Polly and Sam had told him last fall—it couldn't have really happened. Or could it have? Joe sighed to himself. He *wanted* it to be true. Maybe if he just played along...After all, what else was there to do on this boring camping trip?

"Sam!" shouted Polly. "I see it! Look!"

Sam and Joe both turned. Polly was staring at the sky. The mist had risen and become low gray clouds.

"I can't see anything," said Sam.

"You have to stand here," said Polly, staring fixedly at the sky.

Sam and Joe went to stand beside her.

Overhead was a break in the grayness. In

puffy letters, like a plane's skywriting, were words, white against the blue sky:

Three feathers for flight.
Three steps to the sky.
Details to follow.

Joe laughed, a little hysterically. "Feathers and skywriting," he said. "It's a pretty expensive joke."

"You'd better be careful, Joe," said Polly. "If you don't believe, the magic will never come to you. Maybe that's it," she added, turning to Sam. "Maybe he's too old. Remember in the Narnia books, how you could get too old to visit?"

The clouds slid over the words in the sky.

"Oh, no," said Polly. "We'll have to remember them. It will be your fault, Joe, if they're gone forever."

"Maybe the words will stay in the sky," said Sam hopefully. "Let's see if it clears."

They waited. It reminded Polly of waiting for water to boil on a stove.

Finally, the clouds parted. The words were gone. It was as if they'd been written in the sand, and the clouds had washed them away like a wave.

Polly sighed.

"I knew it," she grumbled. "We have to *remember* what it said…Either that, or we've missed the magic altogether because Joe was being a grownup…Three feathers for flight. Three stairs…"

"Steps," said Sam. "Three steps to the sky."

"Details to follow," said Joe, shaking his head. "Whatever that means."

"Hey," said Sam. He pointed up. "What's that?"

Joe and Polly looked. Circling overhead was a paper airplane about the size of the feathers. It spiraled lower and lower until it landed smoothly at their feet. Stamped in gold across the wings were the words AIR MAIL.

Joe gulped and closed his eyes.

Sam picked up the paper airplane. He glanced at Polly, who nodded. Sam unfolded the paper. He could nearly see through it. The thin page was blank, except for a slight mistiness.

A cool breeze ruffled the paper. The mistiness shifted.

Joe shivered and opened his eyes. "Is it the details?" he asked.

"It's nothing," said Sam.

"Yet," said Polly. "We have to figure out how to make the words show up."

"It's something in the air," said Joe. He gave a little laugh. "*Air* mail."

Polly ignored him. She held the paper up. It seemed to disappear between her fingers as the mistiness gathered into puffy white letters. The letters stood out against the blue sky like clouds.

The words from the sky were there, plain as day. And beneath them were new words:

To help a lonely hero, the three steps are:

1. Fly by wind
2. Fly by feather
3. Fly by night

Helpful hints:

- Listen and follow.
- Watch for whom the wind brings.
- The feathers show the way.

"Not very exact details," said Joe.

"Well, I feel a little better," said Polly. "I like having something in writing."

"Fly by wind," said Joe. "How are we supposed to do that?"

"Maybe we should hang-glide," Sam suggested eagerly.

"Oh, *yeah*," said Polly. "I can just see Mom and Dad telling us to go ahead and hang-glide." She started to lower the paper.

"Wait," said Joe. Polly lifted the paper back up against the sky. Joe read the words again.

"I wonder who the lonely hero is," he said.

Sam didn't care about the details. "I wish it told us what to do. I want to fly *now!*"

"It does say 'three feathers for flight,'" said Polly, lowering the paper.

Sam held his feather in front of him, the plumed tip turned to the sky. "I want to fly," he said.

Nothing happened.

"Try saying 'wish,'" Polly suggested.

"I *wish* to fly," said Sam. He turned the tip down. "I *wish* to fly!"

Nothing again. Sam looked at the feather. He thought about sticking it in his hair or holding it in his mouth.

"Try asking the air," said Joe. "Or the wind. It has to be more about the wind or the air than about wishes."

"O Wind," began Sam. He held the feather up again. "Help me fly."

The wind didn't answer with words, just a gentle gust that told them nothing.

"I guess we have to wait," said Polly, folding

the paper back into an airplane.

"And 'watch for whom the wind brings,'" intoned Joe. He held his hand out for the airplane. Polly reluctantly handed it over. Joe pressed the plane's wings together, then carefully tucked it into his back pocket.

Sam was still frowning at his feather.

"What's the matter *now*?" said Polly.

"Well," said Sam, "it's just, this time... this time...we're going to do something that I really, *really* want."

"What *I* want," said Joe, "is to know why we got the feathers. Is it really to save a lonely hero? And how are feathers going to help?"

He was looking out at the newly green hills and valleys below. "The last two times there was a reason for the magic that wasn't completely clear from the message. How much can we trust it?"

He looked at Sam and Polly. Then he shrugged and headed toward the narrow path that led back down the mountain.

CHAPTER TWO

Waiting

The air was fresh and crisp as Polly and Sam followed Joe.

They started down the narrow, twisting path between the rocks. Then they had to stop and put their feathers into their back pockets so they could use their hands for balance and for holding on to the rocks. The feathers looked like tails, wagging behind them.

The kids reached the regular trail, which was marked with yellow paint. Here, the trees were dressed in the lacy leaves of early spring.

Sam stopped to watch a robin. It flapped its wings and then caught the wind and glided along. Sam wondered what it felt like.

"We'd better hurry," called Joe from ahead. "Mom and Dad said to be back by twelve."

Sam ran to catch up with Joe and Polly. He was already excited about the camping trip, but now he was even *more* excited.

The day the kids' spring holiday had started, their father had decided to take some time off. "How about a camping trip? I don't get to see you kids enough," he had said.

"Isn't it a little early to go camping?" Mom had asked.

"Not at all," Dad answered. "It will be a family adventure!"

"It will be a disaster," Joe had predicted to Polly and Sam. "They don't have a clue how to camp."

Nevertheless, the whole family had set out with two tents and a lot of food. They had arrived too late in the afternoon to make camp on Horse Mountain. Instead, they spent the first night of the camping vacation in a motel.

They left the motel early in the morning and headed back to Horse Mountain. The station wagon pulled into a nearly empty parking lot, and Dad had taken a vote whether to go hiking first or to set up a campsite right away. Hiking had won.

Now Mom and Dad were waiting in the little cabin where trail maps and information were set up in neat rows on wooden tables. They were talking to a tanned young man with curly dark hair and a baseball cap turned backward.

Sam, Polly, and Joe stood behind their parents, listening to the conversation.

"I'm sorry," the man was saying, "the campgrounds are closed. We can't let you stay here."

"But the guy I talked to last week said there would be no problem," Dad said. "Maybe I should speak to *him*." Dad was talking very nicely, but Sam, Polly, and Joe all knew that tone. It was his "I'm trying not to scream at you even though you are driving me crazy" voice.

The young man seemed oblivious to the brewing storm, but Mom knew that tone, too. "Come on, Harry," she said. "We can go on another hike and just go home. We don't really need to go camping."

Dad looked as if he were counting to ten in his head. "We are going camping," he said, sounding as stubborn as Sam sometimes felt.

"I know!" the young man said brightly. "I have just the place for you. Hold on one sec. I'll give them a call."

Dad made a noise of agreement that sounded like "hmmph." Joe saw Mom shake her head, ever so slightly, and glance up at the log ceiling.

The young man was behind the desk in a flash. He began pressing the phone buttons with a flourish, his eyes sparkling. Polly thought he was terribly cute. Sam was looking at him, too. He nudged Polly.

"There are wings on his hat," he whispered.

"What?" said Polly. The young man was talking quietly on the phone, and she was trying to hear what he was saying.

"Wings," said Sam.

Polly frowned and tore her eyes away from the man. "What are you talking about?"

"That...man...has...wings...on...his... hat," Sam said slowly.

"Oh," said Polly. She looked at the white shape stitched on the side of the man's baseball cap. It did look like a wing. The man turned his head, and she saw there was one on the other side as well. But she didn't see what the big deal was. "So?"

"It's a *sign*," said Sam. "We got feathers, we're supposed to fly, and he has wings on his hat."

Sam's words fell into place like puzzle pieces. "Ahh," said Polly. She felt as if she were waking up from a dream.

"What are you talking about?" asked Joe, leaning toward them.

"He has wings on his hat," said Polly, tipping her head in the direction of the man whispering into the phone.

Joe studied the man. There *were* wings on his hat. "Maybe it's some kind of ranger symbol," he said. "Just because some things are magic doesn't mean *everything* is."

"I think we should go wherever he says," said Sam.

"Yeah," said Polly. "It's like following the feathers."

"Listen and follow," said Sam excitedly.

"Maybe," said Joe.

The man looked up from the phone and saw the kids staring at him. He winked.

Polly blushed. They all looked away, pretending to be interested in the cabin walls.

"There *is* something funny about him," said Joe out of one corner of his mouth.

Just then, the man hung up. "It's all settled," he said. "I'll give you directions. It's not far, and it's a great campground. Well, it's really an orchard, but the farmer lets people camp there in the spring and summer before the apples are ripe. It's called Zephyr's Orchard. You'll love it."

"Thank you so much," said Mom. "You've been very helpful"—she peered at the name tag pinned to the man's shirt—"Herman."

The man laughed and handed Mom a piece of paper with directions and a small map.

"Nice feathers," Herman said as the kids walked out.

The wind ruffled the trees as they headed to the parking lot. Their car was the only one there. They reached the old station wagon, and Dad sighed. "Maybe we should give up on this whole camping idea."

"*No!*" Sam, Polly, and Joe said, a little too loudly.

"We *have* to go," said Sam.

"Yes," said Polly. "It's good for us."

"Yeah," Joe added. "You know, doing a family thing all together."

Dad looked at them in surprise. Mom smiled.

"Well, at least you all agree for once," said Dad.

"I think it would be very nice to go camping," said Mom.

"It would be *wonderful!*" said Polly. She knew if everyone was excited about it, Dad would get excited as well. "Please, Daddy?"

"I *really* want to," said Sam.

Joe couldn't bring himself to beg, so he just looked at Dad with a hopeful expression.

Dad looked at their eager faces. Then he looked at Mom.

"It's up to you, Harry," she said. "This is your trip."

Dad smiled. "We're off on an adventure!" he said. He raised his fist to the sky. "To Zephyr's!"

Sam, Polly, and Joe raised their fists, too.

"To Zephyr's!" they shouted.

CHAPTER THREE

Zephyr's Orchard

Sam, Polly, and Joe had to take the feathers out of their pockets to get into the car.

"Wow," said Mom. "Those are great feathers. Where on earth did you get them? They don't look real."

"They're real," Polly said.

"They came from the sky," said Sam.

"Who's going to navigate for me?" said Dad from the driver's seat.

"I think it's best if *I* do," said Mom, opening the directions.

Sam looked over her shoulder.

The paper had doodles of clouds with faces blowing lines of wind.

Polly and Joe saw it, too.

Mom looked back at them all leaning over her seat.

"Seat belts," she said.

The three kids leaned back and put their seat belts on. The car pulled out of the parking lot.

Waiting was never easy.

A few hours later, they came to a crossroads in a valley. The car slowed.

Mom consulted the directions. "Left. It should be along here in just a few miles."

The car turned and reluctantly climbed a hill. At the top, to the right, was a big wooden sign partly hidden by ivy.

"I think this is it!" said Mom. "Turn in."

Suddenly, the sun streamed down and the wind gently blew the ivy back from the sign. They read the faded red letters:

ZEPHYR'S ORCHARD
Apples that blow you away...
camping off-season

"It's a sign!" said Sam when he read the word *blow*.

"It certainly is," said Dad, turning the car down the dirt road. "And someone has a sense of humor."

Sam didn't know what Dad was talking about. He didn't see anything funny at all. Polly and Joe looked at each other and rolled their eyes. Mom chuckled.

"Zephyr's Orchard, here we come!" said Dad.

The car rolled forward slowly. The kids undid their seat belts and pressed their noses against the window. Neat rows of trees with new leaves stretched out to one side.

"It's a strange place to camp," said their mother.

"Camping is camping! Look at those new leaves!" exclaimed Dad.

They pulled up beside a little blue house.

A wild-haired person came out and waved.

Sam, Polly, and Joe hung out by the car as their parents made the camping arrangements.

Joe pulled the paper airplane out of his pocket. He unfolded it and held it up to the sky. They only got to look at it for a moment before their parents were heading back to the car.

"We'll talk about it tonight," said Joe with a nod toward the paper as he folded it back up.

"Okay," Polly said. "And we'll figure out what it all means."

Sam didn't say anything. He couldn't understand why Joe and Polly wanted to figure out what everything meant.

"Off we go!" said Dad as Mom shooed them into the car.

They drove until they reached a sign that said PARKING. There were no other cars around. They unpacked in the golden light of the setting sun.

It took several trips, but at last all their camping stuff was spread beside a picnic table near one of the bigger trees. There were two tents: a new one, which Sam, Polly, and Joe were sleeping in, and an old one that had belonged to their grandparents.

Joe pored over the directions for setting the kids' tent up. The light was fading. Sam and Polly pulled the poles and stakes out of nylon bags and laid them on the ground.

"Let's start," said Sam.

"I want to see how it all fits," said Joe.

"We *know* how it all fits," said Polly. "We put tents up every day for a whole week last summer when we were camping with Uncle Linc and Aunt Jan."

"This one might be different," said Joe.

Sam and Polly looked over at their parents, who were struggling with their old tent. Dad liked directions as much as Joe, but there weren't any for the old tent. Sam hoped Mom and Dad wouldn't start fighting over it. He hated it when his parents disagreed.

"All right," said Joe. "I think I've got it."

Joe slotted poles, and Sam and Polly arranged the tent in a big square on the ground.

At loops around the edge of the tent, they banged stakes into the ground with rocks. Finally, they pushed the poles through other loops and raised the tent.

A shout made them look over to where their parents' tent was collapsing in a heavy green heap.

"We'll help you," Joe called.

"No, no," said their father. "I'll put it up in a jiffy."

"I think help is a good idea," said Mom.

Dad frowned. "No, I can do it."

Joe stood uncertainly. Something about this felt familiar. He grinned—he'd said the same thing before himself. In fact, he could remember times when Polly and Sam had said it, too.

"We need to start a campfire," said Mom. "That is, if we want dinner and some light. Harry, I think I'd feel more comfortable if *you* did the fire and we let the kids put up the tent."

Dad looked at the fallen tent in frustration. Then he gave in. "I'll get that fire going," he said.

It took some doing, but the old tent went up at last. It was dark now, but the campfire made a golden glow over the apple trees and tents.

"We're getting another new tent before the *next* camping trip," said Dad, putting hamburgers on the campfire grill. "One with directions."

After dinner and stories by the campfire, Dad handed Joe the big flashlight. "We're going to stay up for a while," said Dad. "But after we go to sleep, you can wake me up if you hear anything strange...or get scared."

"I won't get scared," scoffed Joe.

"Well, Sam or Polly might," said Dad, looking at them. "If anyone gets scared, your mom and I will be here."

"Okay," said Polly. She didn't *think* she'd get scared, but it made her feel better anyway.

Inside the tent, Joe set up the flashlight in the corner. The kids put on their pajamas, shivering, and climbed into their sleeping bags.

Joe had taken the paper airplane out of his jeans pocket. Now he unfolded it.

The misty paper was blank.

"Shoot," said Joe. "I forgot that we'd need the sky to be able to see it."

"*I* remember the important parts," said Polly.

"Three feathers for flight," said Sam.

"Three steps to the sky," said Polly.

Joe nodded as he refolded the paper

"And somehow we have to find and help some lonely hero guy," Joe said. "How are we going to do that?"

"Fly!" said Sam. "We're supposed to fly."

"But how?" asked Joe.

"We have to listen and follow," said Polly. "And watch who the wind blows in."

"And let the feathers show the way," added Sam.

"We listened and followed the guy with wings on his hat," said Joe. "What was his name?"

"Herman," said Polly with a happy sigh.

Joe frowned in thought. "Hermes!" he exclaimed.

"What?" said Sam.

"He's one of the Greek myth guys," replied Joe. "He had a hat with wings. And shoes with wings, too."

"Yeah," said Polly. "I remember him from one of our books."

Just then, Mom called out for them to turn off the light. Joe flipped the switch on the flashlight. Everything was dark except for the glow through the tent where the campfire was.

The three kids were quiet. The campfire crackled and their parents' voices were a low hum.

Soon only Joe was awake, listening to the night sounds. His eyes stayed open until after his parents had put out the fire and gone to bed.

As he began to fall asleep, he heard a sound like a car in the distance. The wind rustled through the new leaves of the apple trees. An owl hooted.

Joe's last thought before he fell asleep was *Maybe the wind has brought someone in*.

CHAPTER FOUR

A Visitor

Sam woke up. His nose was cold. He could hear his parents talking to someone outside. He sat up in his sleeping bag. The air was chilly, but the light was bright through the side of the tent.

Sam rubbed his eyes, yawned, and looked around sleepily. Polly was stirring a little. Joe had his head under his pillow and was as still as a log.

Sam felt around for his clothes. They were cold and damp. Staying inside his sleeping bag, he pulled the jeans and sweatshirt on over his pajamas. Then he climbed out of the sleeping bag and crawled over to the tent opening, where he put on his socks, shoes, and jacket.

Sam unzipped the tent flap and squeezed out. He blinked slowly in the sparkling sunshine and then sleepily pulled the flap zipper closed. He yawned again. What had he dreamed about last night? It had been something good.

"Sam," called his dad. "Come and meet a fellow camper. She's here studying owls."

"Oh," said Sam. He peered without interest at the lady sitting at the picnic table with his parents.

Dad chuckled. "Sam's not at his best first thing in the morning."

The owl lady had a low laugh. "I understand that."

Mom handed Sam a plastic cup filled with orange juice. Then she led him over to the campfire, which was warm and blazing. It was strange to have a fire going in the day, but

Sam was happy to feel the heat.

Sam studied the stranger over the edge of his cup. She was older than his parents and had funny round glasses and dark hair streaked with gray. She had on a white shirt, jeans, a leather vest, and a hat with a wide brim. Sam liked the feathers stuck in the hatband.

A breeze blew at the fire, making it crackle.

Suddenly, Polly burst out of the tent, bundled in a sweater and jacket, her hair in tangles.

"I need to go to the bath—" She saw the owl lady and stopped. "Oh."

"And this is our daughter, Polly," Dad said to the owl lady.

Polly smiled politely and turned to her mother. "Um, Mom..."

"I'll take you up to the house," Mom said. "We need some more water anyway."

Polly and Mom headed off.

Dad fixed Sam a bagel with cream cheese without interrupting his conversation with the owl lady. Sam stared at the fire and half listened as he slowly started to wake up.

The owl lady didn't just study owls. She studied wars and art and was a school librarian. Sam thought it was interesting for a woman to study wars. His father seemed to think so, too, because he asked a lot of questions. Then the owl lady talked about a lot of other jobs she'd done, some of which Sam had never heard of.

Mom and Polly came back carrying containers of water. Polly had pulled her hair out of her eyes and into a ponytail. She fixed herself a bagel and came and sat next to Sam by the fire.

"Should we wake Joe up?" asked Polly. "And take a look at the air mail again?"

Just then, Joe stumbled out of the tent. Everyone looked at him.

"Back in a sec," he said, smiling sheepishly and heading into the trees. A feather waved from his back pocket.

Polly nudged Sam, and he smiled in spite of himself. Sam was about to say something about the owl lady when Joe came back.

He pulled his feather out of his back pocket and sat down beside Polly and Sam at the fire. He pushed his hair out of his eyes and twisted the feather between his fingers. Sam decided it wasn't the best time to say anything. Joe was *really* not a morning person.

Joe muttered something.

"What?" said Polly.

"Juice," said Joe.

"I'll get it," said Sam. He jumped up. He did feel much more awake now.

Sam held a cup of juice out to Joe. Joe carefully set the feather down and took the cup.

"Thanks," said Joe. He lifted the cup to his lips and drank all the juice in one long gulp. He held the cup out to Sam. "More," he said.

Sam didn't like having to get Joe another cup of juice, but it was easier than arguing. He went and poured more orange juice into the cup and brought it back to Joe.

Polly picked up the feather. She held it up to the light. "Let's get the air mail," she said.

"Not here," said Joe, looking toward the grownups at the picnic table. "Wait—who's that?"

"She's an owl-studying lady," said Sam. "And a librarian, and a lot of other things I can't remember."

"I heard an owl last night," said Joe. "And a car, and...wind." Joe looked over at the owl lady again. She was talking with their parents. "Watch for whom the wind brings...," he said.

"Do you think she's magic?" asked Sam.

"Maybe," said Joe. "At least Mom and Dad seem to think so. They look like they've had a spell put on them."

Sam glanced over at the table. Mom and Dad were both leaning toward the owl lady, who was talking in a low, calm voice. They kept nodding their heads or laughing at what she said. The owl lady sometimes smiled slightly, but she never laughed.

Sam shifted uncomfortably. He didn't like the idea of his parents being bewitched.

Joe noticed Sam's worried look. "I'm just kidding, Sam. Magic doesn't happen to grown-up people. They just like her. Right, Polly?"

"Huh?" Polly looked up from the feather that she'd been twirling between her hands. "What?"

Joe rolled his eyes. "Geez, you're going to hypnotize yourself doing that."

"I am *not*," said Polly, frowning. But she did feel a little weird.

"Could you *really* hypnotize yourself?" asked Sam.

"Sure," said Joe. "Polly should be careful. She might believe it if we tell her she's a skunk or something right now."

Sam snickered at the thought.

Polly punched him in the arm. But not very hard. She looked over at her parents to see if they'd noticed.

Polly gasped, her eyes wide open. She grabbed Joe.

"Hey, watch it!" he said, holding the orange juice cup away.

Polly pointed with the feather. "The owl lady! She...look!"

Sam and Joe looked over. Everything seemed to be the same as it had been five minutes before. The three adults were drinking coffee and talking.

But Polly was clearly seeing something different. Her mouth opened and closed like a hungry baby bird's, and her eyes were shining.

"Maybe she really did hypnotize herself," said Sam, wondering how they were going to undo it.

Joe was obviously thinking the same thing. He clapped his hands in front of Polly's face. "Snap out of it, Pol," he said.

Polly shook her head. "I'm not hypnotized!" she snapped. "Don't you *see?*"

"See what?" asked Joe.

"The owl lady," said Polly. "She's sort of shining, and has a helmet on and armor and an owl on her shoulder."

Sam and Joe looked back at the table, then at each other. Joe shook his head. "You're cracking up, Pol," he said. "Too much magic has gone to your head." He glanced at Sam. "You should be careful—you might be next."

Sam couldn't tell if Joe was kidding or not. He didn't like the thought of going crazy.

"Really, you guys," said Polly in a pleading voice. "How can you *not* see it?"

"You're not joking?" said Joe.

"*No!*" said Polly.

Her shout made the adults turn and look at them.

"Everything okay?" called Mom.

The owl lady peered at them through her glasses. Then she slowly smiled and nodded at them.

Joe and Sam tried to see what Polly was seeing, but they couldn't.

Polly poked Joe with her feather. Suddenly, Joe saw the area around the picnic table blaze with light. The light was coming from the owl lady! Then, just as suddenly, everything was normal again.

"We're fine," Joe said, his voice cracking.

"Fine," he repeated in a deeper voice. But he was shaking his head, trying to figure out what he'd seen.

"What's the matter?" asked Sam. "You sound funny."

Polly smirked. "He saw *her*," she said. "Right?"

"Well," said Joe carefully, "I saw something."

"Oh, no," said Sam. "Please don't *both* be crazy."

"We're not crazy," said Joe. "We just have to—wait. I know!"

He snatched the feather from Polly's hands and looked over at the table. Again it blazed. The owl lady glowed majestically. Joe saw a spear leaning up against the picnic table as well. The owl lady looked back at him. She grinned and winked. Joe caught his breath. He smiled back until she looked away.

"Wow," he said. "The feathers will show the way." He handed the feather to Sam. "You look."

Sam took the feather and turned to the table.

The lady blazed up in golden light. Her armor and helmet reflected the sun. The huge white owl on her shoulder looked at Sam. Its eyes were as round as a full moon. The round eyes blinked. The owl nodded its head.

Sam nodded back.

Then the golden light and the owl were gone.

Joe was holding the feather again. "I think she's Athena," he said. "The Greek goddess of wisdom."

CHAPTER FIVE

Athena

"How do you know she's the goddess of wisdom?" Polly asked.

"She has a spear and a helmet, just like in the pictures in our Greek myth book," said Joe. "I bet *she* knows what's going on."

"Maybe she'll turn us into birds," said Sam.

"Maybe she'll tell us who the lonely hero is," said Polly.

Just then, their mom called out, "Joe, is that one of those feathers you found yesterday? Ann wants to take a look at it."

Joe looked up and was struck by the goldenness of the goddess again. It was a bit overwhelming. He looked away.

"Bring it over," called Dad. He turned to the goddess in disguise. "These feathers are pretty incredible. I don't know what kind of bird they're from."

Joe looked terrified.

"We'll come with you," said Polly.

Sam nodded.

"I have an idea," said Polly. She took the feather from Joe, who instantly felt both better and worse. Polly pulled her sleeve down and put the feather in her hand with the cloth between the feather and her skin. "It works," she said. "I mean, it's great to see the goddess and all that, but it makes it hard to think."

"Yeah," said Joe.

They stood up and walked toward the picnic table. Everything seemed completely normal, although now that they knew what they were looking at, they all could sense the power around the goddess. What surprised Joe was that their parents had seemed to feel it all along.

"May I have it?" asked the owl lady, holding her hand out for the feather while looking Polly in the eye.

"Why are you holding the feather in your sleeve, Polly?" Mom asked. She leaned over to the owl lady. "Kids are so funny."

The goddess smiled without shifting her gray eyes from Polly's brown ones.

Polly found herself smiling back and feeling less afraid. It helped that the goddess looked fairly normal without the feather-sight. She reminded Polly of one of those teachers who is stern but fair and who you desperately want to impress.

The three kids watched as Athena—none of them could think of her as "Ann"—stroked the feather.

"Ah, yes, I wondered who would get them," she murmured very softly. She looked searchingly at the worried faces of the children, then turned to their parents. "This is from an endangered creature. One that many people think is extinct."

There was a moment of silence. Finally, Dad said, "That's amazing."

"The kids found three of those feathers," said Mom. "Out on Horse Mountain, on one of the trails there." She raised her eyebrows at Joe. "Where was it you said you got them from? The sky?"

Joe gulped. "Yeah. I mean, they just came right down."

"It's possible the bird's alive," said Dad.

"Maybe the feathers fell from a flying bird, or maybe the kids were near a nest…" Mom's voice trailed off. "It just seems as if you might be able to find it."

Athena nodded. "Perhaps I could take the children, and they could show me where they found them." She turned her gray gaze on Sam, Polly, and Joe. "You wouldn't mind, would you?"

"Oh, no," said Polly.

"Uh-uh," said Sam.

"We don't mind at all," said Joe.

The gray eyes turned to their parents. "Can you lend them to me? Just for the day? Or do you want to come as well?"

Mom and Dad looked at each other and had a conversation with their eyes.

"In the name of science, you may borrow the children," Dad said in his announcer's voice.

Mom smiled.

The three kids groaned.

"Da-ad," said Polly.

Dad grinned and wiggled his eyebrows. Then he shook his head and was serious. "I think it would be a great thing to help make a difference. And you're going to learn a lot. The real question is, can Ann put up with you all? Especially on that long car ride back to the mountain."

"It should be no problem," Athena said. "I'm used to keeping people in line."

"If you say so," said Mom. She looked at her children and wagged a finger at them. "You guys are going to be on your best behavior, right? That means no whining, no bossing, and *no* bickering."

"Yes, ma'am," said Joe with a salute.

"Well, okay, then," said Mom. "They're all yours, Ann. And thanks for giving us a free day."

"I just have to pull some things together," the goddess said. "I'll be back in half an hour or so."

Sam sighed. He felt as if he were flying already. It was starting, and who knew what was going to happen.

The kids straightened their tent up in five minutes. They put the paper airplane and the remaining two feathers, carefully wrapped in one of Sam's T-shirts, into Joe's backpack. Athena had kept the feather that they had shown her.

"I guess that means we've reached one of the steps," said Joe.

Mom made them sandwiches while their father put away the breakfast stuff. Joe grabbed a bagel and ate it while they waited for Athena to return. It had grown warm in the sun, and they took off their jackets and held them. They were jittery with excitement.

Joe pulled out the air mail message. He held it up to the sky when their parents weren't looking. It teased the kids with its magical-looking cloudy words, but didn't tell them anything new. So they lay back beside an apple tree shadow and watched the few clouds in the sky.

"What kind of tent do you think she has?" Polly wondered.

"Probably she doesn't have one, and she can just get anywhere instantly," said Joe.

"Like on *Star Trek*," said Sam.

"Yeah," said Joe.

"I think she has a beautiful tent made of velvet and silk with candles in it," said Polly dreamily.

Joe shook his head. "Candles? No way—the whole thing would burn down."

Suddenly, a voice came from above them. "Ready?"

It was Athena. She had on sunglasses and was holding a leather bag with papers sticking out of it.

Sam, Polly, and Joe all scrambled up. Polly and Joe were both very embarrassed to have been caught talking about her.

"Let's go," said Athena. She strode off between the trees and didn't look back.

The kids ran to catch up with her. They all wanted desperately to ask questions, but it didn't feel like the right time. So they just trotted along beside her.

Finally, Sam spoke up. "I hope you know a shortcut, because it was a really long ride yesterday."

"Shhh, Sam," Polly hissed.

"I just figured since she's a...you know," Sam whispered, "that she's got to have a good way of getting around, like we said."

Athena looked over her shoulder. "Yes, I have a shortcut," she said, an amused note in her voice. "And I do have a somewhat different way of traveling. But it is not like *Star Trek*."

"Oh," said Sam. "I'm sorry."

"Don't worry," Athena said. "I think you'll find it quite exhilarating."

"What does that mean?" asked Sam. "Ex-zill-erating?"

"It means 'thrilling and exciting,'" said Joe. "Now be quiet."

"Oh, no," said the goddess. "Questions are good. A combination of question and observation is at the root of almost all learning."

"Do you really want us to show you where we found the feathers?" asked Polly.

"I don't think that will be necessary," Athena said. "I sent them."

"You *did?*" said Polly, surprised.

"Yes," said Athena. "But they chose you as the best people to help."

"The feathers chose us?" asked Sam.

Athena nodded. "And the winds chose, too."

"Does that mean you'll help us now?" asked Joe.

"Actually," said Athena, "*you* will be helping *me*. I can change the mortal world only so much. But I can guide humans in certain directions if the cause is just."

"How are you going to guide us?" asked Sam.

"I will take you to a friend, a mortal, who can help you," said the goddess.

"Where is he—or she?" asked Joe. "How long will it take? I'm not sure it will be okay with Mom and Dad."

"Don't worry about them," Athena said. "I will take care of the details."

"Who's the lonely hero?" asked Polly. She couldn't believe they'd forgotten the most important question.

"Ah," said the goddess. "*That* you will have to discover on your own."

They reached the edge of the orchard. A little ways away from the family's old station wagon was a silver truck.

"Cool," said Joe. "Is that yours, um,

ma'am?" The goddess made him nervous, which, in turn, made him feel stupid. "What *should* we call you?" he blurted out, and immediately regretted it.

"I assume you know my real name," Athena said, her gray eyes dancing with laughter.

Joe nodded. So did Sam and Polly.

"Then you may use it," she said. "And, yes, that is my vehicle."

They reached the shining silver truck.

"Climb in," said Athena with a knowing smile. "And be careful."

Joe reached out to run his hand along the gleaming paint. The moment his finger touched it, the metal beneath his hand became warm.

CHAPTER SIX

Another World

Joe was touching the silvery flank of an enormous horse. The horse snorted, and Joe quickly withdrew his hand. Instantly, it turned back into a truck.

Sam and Polly were inside it, their eyes as big as saucers.

Joe felt a hand on his shoulder. He tensed up and then relaxed. He looked up into the goddess's face.

"I won't let anything bad happen to any of you as long as you are with me," she said. "I swear on the River Styx, the strongest oath that anyone in my family can give."

Joe gulped and reached out again.

The metal became flesh. The horse whinnied. Joe stroked its strong side. Another horse stood beside the one he was patting. They were harnessed to a wooden chariot with two wheels. There was one funny thing about it: it had an upholstered seat that looked as if it had come out of a car—maybe even the truck.

The rest of the chariot had been painted silver and was as shiny as the truck had been. There were carvings on the side of it. Joe could make out a tree and a spider web.

Sam and Polly leaned back against the seat. Beyond them the sky was a vivid blue. One very white cloud stretched out across it like a sleeping man. There were rows of apple trees, just as in Zephyr's Orchard, but the leaves were fuller and brighter green, and golden yellow apples hung plump from the branches.

The family's station wagon was nowhere in sight.

Joe climbed onto the seat beside Sam and Polly.

"Scoot over," he said.

They made room for him.

"Where's Athena?" asked Polly.

Suddenly, the giant white owl appeared on the chariot in front of them. It spread its wings and disappeared.

It reappeared on Sam's shoulder. It was heavy, and Sam could tell that its talons were sharp, but it was being careful not to hurt him. He felt a bubble of joy rise into his throat.

"I think she likes you," Athena said, appearing beside the chariot in much the same way as the owl had. She had on her goddess garb of helmet and armor over a long white sleeveless tunic. Sandals laced up her calves, and she still had her sunglasses on and the bag of papers over her shoulder. She nodded at Sam. "You must be a wind dreamer."

"A *what?*" said Sam.

"Someone who dreams of flying, of catching the wind and sailing on it," she answered.

Sam nodded. "I do dream of flying." He looked at the goddess shyly. "I'm going to get to fly, aren't I?" he asked.

"In more ways than one," Athena assured him.

Sam let out a sigh of relief.

The goddess's brightness was less startling but no less beautiful in the equally bright landscape.

Athena took off the helmet and unbuckled the chest plate. "These are really only good for battle," she said. "And impressing people. Were you impressed?"

The kids nodded.

"Good," Athena said, smiling. "It's nice to know it still works."

She went behind the chariot. Sam, Polly, and Joe twisted around to see what she was doing. She put her things away in some kind of compartment at the back. Then she pulled out a long white piece of cloth.

Athena wrapped the cloth around her waist like a sash, looping and tucking it so that it fell gracefully over her body. Then she climbed into the chariot and sat easily between Polly and Joe.

"I have modernized a little," she said, taking up the reins. "Chariot seats used to be very uncomfortable. When they had any seat at all."

"Where are we?" Joe asked.

"This is a place between times," said Athena. She paused, listening to the wind. "We should leave now." She scanned the sky and the horizon.

The horses stamped their feet and snorted.

"Should *we* do anything?" asked Sam.

"Just hold on!" answered Athena. She adjusted her sunglasses and snapped the reins.

The horses leapt forward—right into the sky.

The kids were pressed back into the seat as they rose. It felt like a plane taking off, except that there was a lot more wind. Their hair blew back, and a rushing sound filled their ears. Sam felt the owl's talons dig in as it held on.

Slowly, they leveled off, and the rushing

sound and wind died down. Sam and Joe both leaned over the edge of the chariot. Through a fine layer of cloud, they could see the world spread out like a crazy quilt of different textures and patterns. It was cool, but it didn't feel like the flying that Sam had imagined.

"Why can't we feel the wind anymore, Athena?" he asked, slightly disappointed.

"Because we're riding on its back, not going against it," said Athena. "Actually, there are four winds. We are traveling with Zephyr, the West Wind. He's the kindest and softest of the wind brothers."

"That's the name of the orchard we're camping at," said Joe.

"Even a wind needs a home," replied Athena.

"Where are we going now?" asked Polly.

"Back in time to visit an old student of mine," Athena answered. "He's a genius and a master of riddles. I think he can give you something you'll need on your quest."

Joe pulled the paper airplane out of his

backpack and unfolded it. He held it up and read the words.

"Are we going to get wings?" he said. "Or be turned into birds?"

"What makes you think that?" asked Athena in a tone like a teacher asking why you liked a book.

"Well, the first step is to fly by wind," said Joe. "Which is what we're doing right now. The second step is to fly by feather. The only way I can think of doing that is to have wings."

Sam stopped stroking the owl's head. "Wings?" he said. "Wings of our very own?"

Athena nodded. "You're right in your guess. And my friend is the one who can give you wings. But you'll have to convince him to do it. He had a very bad experience. He gave his son a pair of wings. And, well, his son didn't listen to his father's advice, and that was the end of him."

"What do you mean 'the end of him'?" Polly asked in a quiet voice.

"Flying is a dangerous thing," said Athena.

"He fell and was killed. It was very tragic."

The three kids were silent, thinking about the story.

"So you understand why he may not want to give you wings," said Athena. "You're all very young, and he may have a hard time believing that you'll listen to him and follow his directions."

"We would listen," said Polly. "Listen and follow." She looked over at Joe.

"It's not me you have to convince," the goddess said. "Uh-oh."

"Is something wrong?" asked Joe.

A bank of dark clouds had risen ahead of them.

"Notus," said Athena, nodding toward the clouds. "I was hoping we could avoid him."

"Who's Notus?" said Polly, her voice wavering.

"The South Wind," said Athena. "When the winds meet, they sometimes fight."

The sound of wind rose around them, but the chariot slowed down as it neared the darkening clouds. The three kids watched in fascinated horror as the clouds boiled and grew until they looked like a man flying toward them headfirst. Water dripped down his face and beard.

"He looks so sad," said Polly.

"Hold on!" Athena shouted.

Suddenly, the chariot dropped. Sam, Polly, and Joe all screamed. They couldn't help it. It was much scarier than a roller coaster. The chariot rose and dropped again.

Sam gripped the side of the chariot, and the owl gripped Sam's shoulder. It pressed against him. Sam could feel damp feathers on his cheek. He shut his eyes.

Joe held on to the other side of the chariot, and Polly hung on to Joe. She wanted to hold on to Athena, but the goddess was busy controlling the plunging horses.

The dark clouds were rushing toward them. The dripping face got bigger and bigger, and the sound was deafening. Just as they were looking the giant wind in the eye, Athena pulled on the reins, and the chariot swung up and to the left.

The chariot bumped along like a ship going over waves. It moved more and more slowly until it stopped. Then it started going backward. The horses bucked and neighed as they were dragged back.

Then the chariot began to spin in the battling winds.

It occurred to Polly that this was what being in a tornado must feel like. Dark and light clouds twisted around each other on every side. Polly was very dizzy, and the force of the spin pressed her against Joe, who kept pushing her away.

"I can't help it!" she screamed in apology. But he didn't hear.

Joe's arm was going to sleep. He was terrified, and that irritated him. He wondered if it was keeping him from being as scared as he should be. He was also wondering how good Athena's promise really was.

Sam opened his eyes for a second. The owl had left his shoulder for Athena's. The bird's beak was open, as if it were telling her something, but Sam couldn't hear anything over the wind. Athena had lost her sunglasses, and her hair whipped around her face.

Then rain hit. The drops came at them like stinging bees. Athena shouted, but her voice disappeared instantly into the howling winds.

Suddenly, a huge bolt of lightning cracked in front of them.

The sky lit up in an explosion of white and purple.

Thunder roared like a lion.

Then everything was dark, and the chariot plunged down.

CHAPTER SEVEN

A Tale

With a gentle bump, the chariot stopped falling. Sam opened his eyes. He was surprised to see that they weren't on the ground. They were on a dense cloud in the gray sky. In the distance, the storm raged on, sheets of rain falling to the earth below.

Sam was shaken and wet. Polly and Joe looked as if they were, too.

The owl fluffed her feathers.

Athena glanced around with a pleased expression on her face. She smiled at the kids. "Having fun yet?" she asked.

Then she pushed her wet hair away and snapped the reins. The chariot surged forward again, right into the clouds.

"What happened?" asked Joe.

"Oh," said Athena, "the lightning was from my father. I hate having to call him, but the winds were fighting so loudly that he was the only one who could hear me. He called Eurus to carry us away. Eurus is the East Wind. He doesn't get called very often."

"I can see why," said Polly as the chariot dipped and rose inside a damp mass of clouds. It was like being in a small sailboat on a choppy lake. Polly shuddered.

Joe was beginning to feel seasick from the motion. He was relieved when they broke through the clouds into a brilliant blue sky. The sun blazed above. Below was turquoise water; ahead was an island, green with trees. Polly could feel her clothes drying in the warmth.

The chariot dropped down in stages, until it came to rest on the edge of a rocky cliff.

"Where are we now?" asked Sam.

"An island called Sicily," said the goddess. She climbed out of the chariot and disappeared. She reappeared behind them, rummaging around at the back of the chariot.

"Hop out," she said.

Joe got out first, shifting his backpack on his shoulders. Polly and Sam followed him. As they stepped away from the chariot, the world changed around them again.

All the colors faded slightly, but they were brighter than back in Zephyr's Orchard. The air was warm, and the sun was shining. The chariot had become a solid wooden wagon, and the horses were a pair of oxen.

In front of them was a low white house with a red roof and wooden shutters. It was perched a small distance away from the edge of the cliff. Around it was a low wall and small trees. A large cow and a goat grazed outside the wall.

A dirt road led away from the house along the cliff edge. It went down to a small city, also made up of white buildings. Larger buildings with columns stood out among the houses, as well as some giant statues.

"Come on," Athena said, wrapping a scarf over her hair as she strode toward the house. The owl flew after her.

The three kids followed slowly, still looking around.

An old man came to the door. He was more than old, Sam thought—he was *ancient*. He used a cane and had wispy hair on his head and a long, wispy white beard. Athena gave him a gentle hug.

"This is Daedalus," she said, putting an arm around the old man's thin shoulders. Then she said each of their names as she pointed to them.

They all smiled shyly.

The old man looked sideways at Athena. "And what is it you want me to do for these children from the future that you cannot do yourself?"

Athena brought her hand to her chest dramatically. "You know I can't get very involved in human affairs," the goddess said.

"Oh, no," grumbled the old man. "Only enough to take sides in wars and turn girls into spiders."

"She deserved it," Athena said.

"I know that," Daedalus replied, "but I'd call that getting too involved in human affairs."

"Maybe," said Athena, "but you know my father prefers us to be careful."

"Yes," said Daedalus. He sighed. "So what is it?"

Athena turned to the kids. "You tell him."

Sam stepped toward the ancient man. "We'd like some wings, please," he said in as polite a voice as he could.

The old man stood very still. They could see his white hair trembling. His eyes watered, and he shook his head.

"That is one thing I will not do," he said, turning away. "Take them home, great goddess. There is nothing I can do here."

"But—" began Polly.

"*No!*" Daedalus said sharply. Then his face softened. "I can't," he whispered.

Sam, Polly, and Joe looked at Athena. She shrugged.

Sam couldn't believe it. His chance to really fly was being snatched right out from under his nose. "Please?" he said, stepping forward. He squared his shoulders bravely. "I'll do whatever it takes."

Polly stepped up as well. "We need the wings," she said. "It's important. We're supposed to do something special. We don't know exactly what yet. But if we don't have the wings, we won't be able to do it at all."

Joe shifted his backpack. He knew he should step in and plead their case, but all he could think about was being hungry. Which made him think about what they'd packed earlier that day. Which made him think about the two remaining feathers wrapped in Sam's T-shirt in the backpack.

Joe took the backpack off and pulled out the T-shirt. Then he unwrapped the feathers. The old man raised his eyebrows. All the wrinkles in his face lifted as well.

Joe took one of the feathers and stepped forward. He held it out to Daedalus.

The old man took it in his gnarled hands. He turned it over. He waved it and watched the colors ripple across it. Then he gently rested it against his cheek and closed his eyes. "Pegasus," he said.

The three kids gasped. They all knew who Pegasus was! It was hard to believe that they'd been carrying around feathers from the very wings of the famous winged horse.

Daedalus nodded at their awed expressions. "Yes," he said. "Pegasus, the symbol of beautiful flight. More lovely than the hawk or the eagle or the owl."

Athena's owl hooted.

Daedalus gave a faint smile. "Lovely in a different way, perhaps," he said. "Birds are meant to have wings. Not horses. And not people." He turned to the three kids and held the feather up. "Do you know what happened to the man who rode Pegasus?"

Sam, Polly, and Joe shook their heads.

"His name was Bellerophon," Daedalus said. "He was a strong young man, a hero, and a wind dreamer. He was also the grandson of a great horse trainer. He had heard of Pegasus, the winged horse that had sprung from the neck of Medusa, and wanted nothing more than to ride him.

"One night, Bellerophon had a dream. In it, Athena came to him and gave him a golden bridle. This bridle would help him tame the swift winged steed. When he woke up, the bridle was beside him, as golden as in his dream.

"Bellerophon was lucky, or perhaps he had the blessing of a certain goddess, for soon Pegasus came to a spring where Bellerophon was drinking. As the creature bent down to sip the sweet water, the young man threw the magic bridle over his head.

"At once, Pegasus, always wild, was tame for Bellerophon. Together, they were swifter, braver, and more reckless than any horse and human had ever been or would ever be. They slew monsters and rescued maidens. And with

Pegasus' help, Bellerophon became a great king.

"But as is the way with fliers, Bellerophon thought he was invincible. He tried to fly into the heavens to take his place with the gods. However, it was not to be. Despite his greatness and the favor of a goddess, Bellerophon was mortal. He did not belong in Olympus, the home of the gods..."

Here the old man stopped and looked at the sky. He shook his head.

"What happened to him?" Sam broke in.

"Only Pegasus made it to Olympus," answered Daedalus. "Bellerophon was thrown down to the earth. He lived, but he wandered, blind and crippled, to the end of his days."

"That's horrible!" exclaimed Polly.

"But true," said Daedalus. "And this is the danger of flight. It is breathtaking to ride the winds and tempting to accept their challenge. The danger itself is exciting!"

Joe shook his head. "Where we come from, people fly all the time, in things called planes. Sometimes they crash, but hardly ever. And I don't think it's because pilots are trying to reach the gods or something."

"I do not know if this is good or bad," said the old man. "I only know what I know from my life. My son was a wind dreamer, and then a flier, and then he was gone. Not so lucky as Bellerophon—to live."

"But Bellerophon was blind and crippled," said Joe. "That doesn't seem fair for someone who'd done so much good stuff."

"And having to live without his best friend," said Polly. "He must have been lonely."

"Lonely," repeated Sam. He looked at Polly and Joe.

"The lonely hero!" they said at the same time.

Daedalus stared at them.

Out of the corner of his eye, Sam saw Athena smiling.

"Bellerophon is the one we have to help," Joe explained to Daedalus. "We didn't know who it was before, but now we do."

Polly reached out and touched Daedalus'

wrinkled hand. “I am sorry about your son,” she said. “But people are all different. We *would* be careful. I promise.”

“I’d watch out for everyone,” Joe said.

“And we’d watch out for Joe,” said Polly.

The old man let out another deep sigh and looked at the feather. “I do not think Bellerophon is the only lonely hero,” he said, as if to himself. He twisted his wispy beard around a finger and looked critically at Athena. She gazed back mildly, waiting for him to make up his mind.

Finally, he turned to the kids. “I will keep this feather,” he said, “and I will make the wings—”

Sam started to say something. The old man raised his hand. “But I am not going to just give them to you. You will have to earn them.”

The three kids cheered.

CHAPTER EIGHT

Wing Building

Daedalus held his hand up again. "You must do exactly as I tell you."

They all nodded.

"You must also help me make the wings so that you understand the power of them," said Daedalus. "It will take some time."

"How much time?" asked Polly. "A few hours?"

The old man chuckled. "A few hours for three pairs of wings? And learning about the wind? And strengthening your bodies? No. It will take a week, maybe even more. We'll see."

Joe shook his head. "I don't know if we can do that," he said. "We're supposed to be back at the campground tonight."

Athena spoke. "I told you I would take care of the details," she said. "I will make sure you return to *your* time at the *right* time."

"Oh," said Joe, looking at Sam and Polly. He shrugged. "I guess it's okay, then."

"I'm glad you approve," said Athena with a slight smile. "It's time for me to go now."

"You're leaving us?" said Polly. "You can't!"

"I can," said the goddess. "But you won't be alone." She put a hand up to the owl on her shoulder. "Stay with these young people," she told her, "and try to stay awake during the day a bit."

The owl hooted and flew to Sam's shoulder. Sam grinned.

"Her name is Clio," said Athena, "after the Muse of history."

"What's a Muse?" asked Sam.

"Look it up," said Athena. The goddess climbed into her chariot. "Listen to Daedalus," she said. "He is a wise man, and I taught him everything he knows."

The three kids, the old man, and the owl watched as she drove off in a cloud of dust. When the dust cleared, the chariot was gone.

"Come," said Daedalus. "We have a lot of work to do."

Sam, Polly, and Joe watched as the old man drew plans in the dirt for a pair of wings.

"You have to know how wings work," said Daedalus. "We will model your wings on those of a predatory bird."

"What's a predatory bird?" asked Sam.

"A bird that hunts and kills things," Joe answered.

"But we don't have to hunt and kill things?" asked Polly. "Do we?"

"No," said Daedalus. "But a predator's wings are the best for what you need to do."

"Whew," said Polly. "I really don't want to kill anything."

Then Daedalus pointed out different parts of the wing and named them: inner primary feathers, outer primary feathers, secondary feathers, covert feathers, and contour feathers. He even got Clio to grudgingly—and sleepily—spread her own wings to demonstrate further how they worked.

The more Daedalus talked, the more energetic he became. He flapped his arms, showing the kids how they'd have to work them once they had the wings on. Soon the kids were on their feet, flapping imaginary wings as well.

Next, Daedalus explained how they would be making the wings. They would cut branches and soak them in water so they could be shaped to mimic the bones of birds' wings. Cloth would be stretched over the branches like skin. Then feathers would be stuck to the cloth with wax.

"It's like a big art project!" said Polly. She liked doing art projects.

Joe groaned. "It's going to take forever!"

"But we get to fly at the end," said Sam.

While they talked, Daedalus drew diagrams

in the dirt. With the diagrams, he showed them how wind currents worked.

"You must learn all of these," he told the children. "We will go over them every day until you take off."

"It's as bad as school," Polly whispered to Joe.

Then Daedalus measured their arms with string. He tied knots in the string to mark the distance from their fingertips to wrists, then wrists to elbows, elbows to shoulders, and shoulders to the middles of their necks.

"The wings will actually be much longer than your arms," he said. "But we will base their size on your own wingspans." He chuckled to himself. "And now we cut the branches. Olive trees are best, for they are Athena's trees and will give you her blessing as you fly."

Luckily, olive trees grew all around Daedalus' house. He chose a tree and, saying a prayer, cut a few branches from it. Then he repeated the process at the next tree and the next.

"I can help," said Joe as the old man became more and more breathless.

"No, no," wheezed Daedalus. "Just take the leaves off the branches I've already cut."

The old man kept chopping and the kids kept stripping leaves until they had a pile of bare branches. They carried the branches to a small stream behind the house. Daedalus showed them how to tie the branches in place so that the water ran over them.

"This way," he said, "the wood will soften. Tomorrow I will trim them to the right sizes. Then we can bend the branches into shape."

"Where are we going to get the feathers?" asked Sam.

"Ah, my child, I have collected feathers for years," said Daedalus. "I have more than enough for three sets of wings."

He looked up at the setting sun.

"Come into the house," said Daedalus. "And take your shoes off at the door. We will rest so that tomorrow we can work."

Joe groaned.

They ate cheese, olives, and delicious bread for dinner. Then the three kids lay down on straw mats on the floor. Daedalus gave them soft, cream-colored blankets, and they used their jackets for pillows. It all felt very strange, but they were too exhausted from the day to let it bother them.

Just as his eyes dropped shut, Joe said, "I feel like I'm dreaming."

Polly and Sam were already asleep.

The next morning, Daedalus gave Sam, Polly, and Joe short white tunics to wear. The simple shifts were soft and worn. The kids tied them at the waist with a rope.

"These belonged to my great-nieces and -nephews," Daedalus told them.

Joe and Sam felt as if they were wearing dresses, but neither of them said anything. Instead, they went to work on the wings.

Over the next four days, they were so busy that there was no time to talk about anything except what they were doing. They fell asleep every night with muscles that ached from tying branches into place and from doing exercises to strengthen their shoulders and arms.

Every meal, the kids ate things they never would have considered even *tasting* at home: lentils, cabbage, and peas, all flavored with onions and garlic. There were also apples, pears, figs, fish, and bread. Clio picked at the food alongside them, never eating much, for she mostly hunted at night.

"I'm kind of starting to like this stuff," Sam said on their third day.

"It's okay," said Polly, wrinkling her nose. "I like the bread. And the fruit."

"I'm hungry. It's food," said Joe.

On the fifth day, Daedalus brought two big bags into the yard, where the cloth-covered wing frames waited.

"They're so beautiful!" Polly exclaimed when she looked into one of the bags.

There were feathers of many different colors, from soft browns and grays to shimmering greens and brilliant reds.

"Some are from griffins," said Daedalus. "The phoenix and the sphinx both gave me a few, too," he said proudly. "It always helps to have some magic feathers up your sleeve, or in this case, on your wings."

As the kids sorted through the feathers, the old man brought a big pot into the yard. He fixed a fire. Then he melted wax in the pot.

"Start with the large feathers at the bottom," Daedalus instructed.

They spent the day attaching feathers to the wings one by one. That night when they went to sleep, they all had blisters on their fingers from pressing the feathers into hot wax.

The next morning, Daedalus woke them early.

"Today," he said, "you fly."

CHAPTER NINE

Rules

It was a bright, breezy morning. Sam, Polly, and Joe dressed in their own clothes, which they'd washed in the stream. Their jeans felt stiff and tight, especially after the light tunics they'd been wearing. Even their shoes felt strange after days of going barefoot.

"I'm afraid practice flights will not be possible," Daedalus said. "You are ready to set off on your search."

"Are you sure?" asked Joe.

"I have taught you twice as much as my son

ever knew," the old man said with a sigh. "I would keep you here longer, but the time has come."

He gave Joe bread and cheese and apples wrapped up in a cloth to carry in his backpack. The sandwiches their mother had packed had long since been eaten and the water drunk, but the kids refilled the bottles with fresh water.

"You must fly across the ocean to Greece," said Daedalus, "where I believe you can find Bellerophon."

"Aren't we *in* Greece?" asked Polly.

"We are on one of Greece's islands," said the old man. "At least right now. But mainland Greece is to the east of here. The goddess's owl knows the way there, so let her lead you. It is possible that she will also be able to make your journey shorter, as she may have some influence with the brothers of the winds."

The three kids brought their wings to the edge of the cliff. Clio flew beside them, hooting encouragement as they pulled the wings, as carefully as they could, along the ground.

The completed wings were giant patchworks of colorful feathers. Each one was more than twice as long as the arm it would rest on. They were fairly light, but the fact that they had any weight at all made both Polly and Joe feel jittery. Only Sam had no fear.

They stopped a few feet from the edge of the cliff. A light breeze playfully ruffled the feathers on the wings. Far below, waves crashed against the rocks.

Daedalus came up behind them. He carried a large cloth bag. Before they put on their wings, Daedalus opened the bag and pulled out strips of linen. He told them to wrap one strip around each ankle.

"Landing is hard on the joints," he explained. "And make sure you bend your knees and run as you land, just like I told you."

The kids nodded. Polly was feeling very nervous, and Joe listened more seriously than ever.

Next they wrapped their wrists, but not too tightly.

"You have to be able to bend them," said Daedalus, "but you need the extra support for when you're holding them rigid."

Finally, it was time for Sam, Polly, and Joe to put on the wings. Daedalus helped them tie the leather bands that held the wings to their wrists, elbows, and shoulders. Leather bands also crisscrossed their chests like double seat belts. Joe wore his backpack in front of him, the straps crossing under it.

The wings were light but awkward. It was like having super-long, stiff arms. The lower edges of the wings nearly touched the ground.

Sam could feel the wind lifting his wings already.

"Can we go yet?" he asked.

"No," the old man said sharply. He pulled three turtle shells out of the bag. They were padded with cloth and had leather straps hanging from them.

"What are they?" asked Joe.

"They go here," said Daedalus, putting one

on Joe's head and tying the straps under his chin. "I don't know how much these will help if you fall, but they should be a little protection if you have a rough landing."

Polly was starting to feel a little sick. She rested her wings on the ground. "Maybe this isn't such a great idea," she said as Daedalus put her helmet on, then Sam's.

The helmets looked pretty funny, but no one laughed.

Joe took a deep breath and blew it out. "We've gotten this far," he said. "We might as well go the whole way." He wondered if Athena's promise to protect them would help them, even if they were no longer with her.

"I want to go," said Sam, edging near the cliffside.

"Get *back* here," said Polly, her helmet sliding down a bit. "We don't have all the rules."

Joe had to smile at that. Polly didn't usually like *other* people's rules.

"Listen carefully. This is very important," the old man said. "You must *not* fly too close to the sun. If you do, the heat will melt the wax that holds the feathers on. They will come loose and you will plunge down."

"The sun's way too far away to do that," scoffed Joe.

Daedalus looked at him. "I speak of what I have seen. Wherever the sun may be, this can indeed happen, so take heed."

"Yes, sir," said Joe, lowering his eyes from the old man's fierce gaze.

"And," Daedalus went on, "do *not* fly too close to the water. If you do, your feathers could get wet and be too heavy to fly. And there are things in the water that will catch you if they can."

"Ick," said Polly.

Joe nodded stoically.

Sam looked out at the cliff edge.

Daedalus went and stood in front of Sam. "You are the one I am most worried about," he said. "You must be the most careful when you fly."

"I *will* be careful!" protested Sam.

"I've heard that before," said Daedalus softly, "with disastrous results. I don't want your deaths on my hands."

Polly shivered. "Don't even say that!" she said. "Maybe we shouldn't go. I don't like the sound of this."

Joe was about to agree with her when the wind hit them from behind.

It was a warm wind and very strong. It caught the three pairs of bright wings like a giant hand and pushed them all toward the edge of the cliff.

Daedalus grabbed Polly and was dragged with her. He tried to catch Joe, but the wind was too strong and Joe was too far away.

Sam, who was closest to the edge, smiled joyfully and spread his wings as Daedalus had showed them. He felt the wind beneath his wings, then felt nothing beneath his feet.

He faintly heard Daedalus' cry: "*Listen!*"

CHAPTER TEN

To Fly

Sam's stomach dropped, but he hardly noticed. He felt the wind and sun against his face. He flapped his wings and looked down as he coasted on a wind current that lifted him higher and higher in the air. He felt no fear looking down at the rocks and white-capped waves, only a feeling of huge joy. He could fly!

Clio pulled up beside him. Sam laughed. Clio tipped her wings and veered off.

Sam tipped his wings and circled around, following her. He was farther from the cliff than he had thought. Sam dropped slightly as he went from one wind current to another, easily adjusting his wings to the wind as he did.

Sam saw Joe circling over the cliff edge. But he couldn't see Polly. Then he heard a shout.

Polly was still on the cliff edge, holding on to Daedalus, who was talking to her. He watched as Polly nodded and slowly let go of Daedalus.

Clio swooped around her as she stepped closer to the edge of the cliff.

"Don't look down!" Joe shouted.

"Come on," Sam called. "It's great!"

Polly looked up and watched as her brothers circled over her head. It wasn't that she was afraid of flying. It was that she was afraid of *falling*. She didn't like looking down and seeing everything far away. That Sam and Joe were both out there, so happy, only made it worse. She was usually brave about everything. How could this be so hard?

Furious with herself, Polly bent her knees and shut her eyes.

"Spread your wings," came a low hooting voice.

Polly spread her wings. She took a deep breath. She heard the waves below and the rustle of olive branches as the breeze touched them. She felt the tug of the wind.

"Let go," came the hooting voice again. "Let go of the ground. Let yourself be light like the wind."

Polly smiled. She let herself fall, tipping her body forward while her wings tipped back.

"Open your wings," the voice ordered immediately. "Open your wings, girl, and flap."

Polly's eyes snapped open. The water was rushing up at her. She screamed, but spread her wings at the same time. The wings caught the wind and the water got farther away as she rose. She flapped, and the wings pushed against the air.

"Here's the current," said the voice. "Go with it."

Polly stopped flapping. She glided along effortlessly and laughed. A hooting gurgle echoed her laughter. She carefully looked over to where the hooting was coming from.

Clio was gliding beside her.

"Were *you* the one talking to me?" Polly asked.

The owl blinked at her and glided calmly away.

Polly smiled. She might have been scared and hesitant, but somehow the owl talking to her made her feel special. Then the wind current dropped and she screamed. She felt a bump as another current picked her up. It took a moment before she felt okay again. Then she looked around carefully once more.

The island was behind her. Already, Daedalus was just a speck on his cliff.

Sam and Joe flew up next to her.

"Are you okay?" Joe called while Sam swooped and dived.

Polly called back. "I'm fine. Daedalus just had to tell me a few things."

"So what did he say?" called Joe.

Polly fell back suddenly with a little shriek.

Then, flapping furiously, she caught up with Joe and glided beside him again. Polly said something too quietly for Joe to hear.

"What?" he called.

"The feather," she shouted breathlessly, "the one we have left."

"What about it?" Joe said. Now it was his turn to drop back. The current blew him so that he had to flap and turn at the same time. When he returned to the good current, Polly had her breath back.

"When we see land, it should be Greece," she said, "and then we'll have to find Bellerophon. Clio won't be able to lead us to him."

Suddenly, Joe was overwhelmed by the difficulty of their task. "Then how are we supposed to find him?" he asked. "Greece isn't a small place."

"The feather—the last feather—will help us find Bellerophon," she yelled as the wind pulled her away. "You just have to hold it. It should tug you in the right direction."

Joe looked down at the backpack strapped to his chest, and his eye caught a flash of something below. "Holy cow!" he said.

"What is it?" asked Polly. She avoided looking down as much as possible.

"Sam!" said Joe. He tipped his wings back and dove.

Polly looked down. Sam was diving, too, his body spiraling. Watching her brother drop toward the shimmering water so far below made her feel sick. She quickly looked back ahead.

"Sam!" Joe screamed as he neared his younger brother.

Sam swooped up, laughing. "Isn't that cool?" he shouted. "I figured out how to do that on my own!"

"Stop it right now!" yelled Joe. "And don't do it again. Mom and Dad will kill me if anything happens to you."

"I'm okay," called Sam. "I'm not going to get hurt."

"Get over here right now," Joe called back. "Or I'll make you!"

But Sam was diving back down to catch a current with a flock of birds. He stayed even with the birds as they skimmed close to the water to catch fish.

Polly took a quick glance down to see what was happening. Her eyes widened. A large tentacle was reaching out of the water.

"Sam!" she screamed. "Look out!"

Sam must have heard something, because he looked up. Polly wanted to point, but the wings wouldn't let her. Instead, she jerked her head frantically.

Sam turned. The tentacle reached farther out of the water and groped around. It caught a bird and pulled it into the sea. The other birds shrieked and flew away like a brown cloud.

Sam flapped his wings. They were heavier and slower than before. Another tentacle reached out of the sea in front of him. Sam turned his body and felt a wing tip touch the water.

Then Joe was beside him. Joe wanted to grab Sam and shake him. But it was not only a bad idea to shake someone while flying, it was impossible. Besides, Sam was looking terrified now.

"Come on!" called Joe.

Sam struggled to right himself. He tipped toward the water again. The tentacle was reaching toward him.

Suddenly, Clio swooped down, screeching and pecking at the tentacle. It slowly sank back into the sea.

Sam gained a little height with Joe's encouragement. Then he caught a breeze and stayed with it.

"You have to keep gliding," called Joe, "until your wings dry."

Sam nodded meekly and caught another wind that took him higher.

Polly was now a ways ahead of them, gliding on a strong current. Finally, they caught up with her.

"Sam," called Polly, "don't you dare do that again. Or I swear I'll disown you."

"Save your breath for flying," shouted Joe.

"I think we still have a long way."

They flew in silence for a while, Clio leading the way. Beneath them was water, and to their left were glimpses of shoreline. At one point they caught sight of a giant school of dolphin leaping joyfully through the waves below. The kids coasted down to watch, careful not to get too close to the water.

The sun slowly crossed the sky until it was behind them.

They were all starting to feel tired. Even though they had been able to glide most of the way, they still had to hold their arms out and be constantly alert to the shifting winds.

"I'm hungry," called Sam.

"Me too," Polly called back.

"When are we going to get there?" called Sam.

"Shut up, you guys," snapped Joe. "I'm trying to figure out how to get the feather out of my backpack without killing myself."

Sam and Polly were silent for a moment in the face of this dilemma. Then Polly spoke. "I bet Clio could get it out for you," she said.

The owl hooted her agreement.

Just then, land came into sight ahead of them.

"We need the feather now," said Joe, "to figure out which way to go." He looked over at Clio, who was coasting silently beside him. She looked back and blinked her round eyes.

"Can you do it?" Joe asked her.

Clio swooped up and away. Joe couldn't see her.

"Careful!" shouted Polly.

"What?" yelled Joe. "What?"

"Not you," called Polly. "Clio!"

Suddenly, Joe felt something heavy land on his head. He was about to panic when Clio hooted.

"Oh, go ahead," he said crossly, embarrassed by his momentary fear.

The owl carefully climbed over his shoulder, digging her claws into the wings' leather straps. Then she was clinging, upside down, to the backpack. Joe struggled to keep balanced as

Clio's weight shifted. It was worse than having someone ride on the handlebars of his bike.

Clio undid the backpack flap with her beak and stuck her head into it. She gave a muffled squawk and pulled her head out.

"It's in the T-shirt," said Joe. "The cloth thing," he added in case she didn't know what a T-shirt was.

Clio hooted and stuck her head into the backpack again.

"Hurry!" said Joe.

Clio brought her head back out, this time with a beak full of T-shirt. She moved away from the backpack opening until the whole T-shirt was out and flapping behind her.

Then a wind current caught Joe unawares. He dipped and tipped. With a shriek, the owl let go of the backpack. The T-shirt dropped from her beak and unrolled in the air.

The feather floated free.

CHAPTER ELEVEN

Lonely Hero

With a swift dive and skillful aim, Sam caught the feather in his mouth! Triumphantly, he swooped back toward Joe and Polly. Then he felt less triumphant. How was he supposed to give the feather to Joe?

"Let it pull you!" shouted Polly. "It will show us the way!"

Just as they glided over the beach, Sam felt the feather tugging him to the right. He nearly opened his mouth to say something, but stopped just in time.

"Don't say anything, Sam!" shouted Joe.

"We'll follow you," called Polly.

Clio swooped beside Sam as he flew along the coast, the feather between his teeth. His brother and sister glided along behind him.

As the sky grew violet ahead, Sam glanced back at the sunset. Against the glowing orange light were the dark winged silhouettes of Polly and Joe. At the center of the sinking sun was a glowing man in a fiery chariot drawn by horses.

Sam looked down. The rolling hills below looked like a sleeping lady, the shoreline curling like locks of hair around her. Sam realized the feather was helping him see these strange things.

The feather gave a tug downward. Sam followed it. Polly and Joe followed Sam.

In the brilliant but fading light, a colorful building with columns and a huge statue came into view. Clio hooted. The statue was Athena. It wasn't as beautiful as the goddess was in real life, but it was definitely her.

"A temple of Athena," Polly said. "Wow."

A man holding a torch was kneeling by the giant statue. He raised his head as he heard the beat of wings over his head. His eyes were clouded like a window covered with frost.

"I bet that's him!" said Polly.

"Let's land," said Joe.

They circled and dropped slowly, trying to stay close to the building. Sam landed first, coasting on a gentle breeze until he could put his feet on the ground, bending his knees as Daedalus had taught. Then he ran as the wind pushed his wings. Gradually, he ran slower and slower, lowering his wings at the same time.

Sam tried to take the feather out of his mouth, but while his elbows bent a little, they couldn't bend all the way. Just as he gave up, he heard a noise and turned to see Joe land.

Joe's bent-knee position was correct, but he tripped over a rock as he ran and fell flat on his face. He looked up and saw Sam watching. Joe managed to stand awkwardly as his little brother ran over to him.

Joe reached forward with a wing.

"Let's see if I can get the feather out of your mouth," he said to Sam.

Joe had just gotten the feather in his hand when he and Sam were knocked over in a flurry of feathers. Polly had run into them, wings outstretched.

"Sorry," she said breathlessly as they lay in a tangled heap. Clio hooted in laughter.

Finally, they unknotted themselves and stood, their wings drooping in the grass. A few feathers were scattered over the ground, and their turtle-shell helmets were crooked.

The kids were standing at the back of the temple. It was bigger than it had seemed from the sky. They looked at each other, and then Joe felt the feather's pull.

"Here we go," he said.

Sam and Polly silently followed Joe. Clio flew ahead of them like a small ghost. They rounded the corner of the temple. The kneeling man with the torch was still in front of the statue. His hair was silver and hung down his back. Trying not to drag their wings, the kids walked toward him.

He raised his head. "Who are you?" he asked.

"We've come to take you to Pegasus," said Sam.

The man raised the torch and bent until his forehead touched the ground.

Alarmed, Polly said, "You don't have to go if you don't want to."

The man lifted his head. "My prayers have been answered," he said. "It was here at Athena's temple that I first dreamed of Pegasus." He turned his face to the breeze. "I wish I had been more content with all I had."

"I don't know how we're going to get you *to* Pegasus," said Joe. "But we'll find a way."

"Pegasus is always here," said Bellerophon, "but out of my reach and out of my sight, for I have none. But *you* can look and see him on a moonless night...Do it. Look up."

They looked up. Sam and Polly saw that the stars had brightened as they talked. Joe saw a sky that twinkled with creatures and people. Pegasus was among them.

"Cool," said Joe. "I never saw the constellations like *this*."

"Like what?" asked Sam.

Then Joe remembered that he was holding the feather. "Look with the feather," he said, giving it to Sam.

Sam stared at the populated sky. He could see Pegasus lying down with his wings folded. It didn't look right.

"Let *me* see!" said Polly.

Reluctantly, Sam gave her the feather.

Polly marveled as the skies opened up like a theater. "Pegasus looks sick," she said. "Maybe he misses Bellerophon."

Clio hooted.

Polly smiled at the stars. Then she said, "Oh!" in a startled voice.

"What?" asked Joe.

"I have an idea," said Polly. She bent over Bellerophon. "I have something that may give you sight," she said gently. "At least into one world."

She pressed the feather into Bellerophon's hand. The old man's face lit up. "I see!" he cried. "I see the sky." He turned and glanced about. "Where are you?" he called. "You who have helped me?"

"You can't see us?" squeaked Sam. It made him feel like a ghost.

"That's what I thought," said Polly. "It can only make him see what it makes *us* see. It only shows the magical things."

"That makes sense," said Joe. "Now how are we going to get Bellerophon up there?" Just the thought made him feel exhausted and aware of how his muscles ached.

"That was the last thing that Daedalus told me," said Polly.

"What?" asked Sam.

"He put a big net in your pack, Joe," said Polly.

Clio hooted and flew to Joe's chest. She dug her claws into the bag and poked her head into it.

Sam laughed.

The owl's white head emerged. Her feathers were ruffled, but she held something in her beak. She pulled it out and laid it on the ground. It was a net of thin, gold threads.

"What are we supposed to do with it?" snapped Joe, who now felt hungry and tired.

"Bellerophon can ride in it while we carry it!" exclaimed Polly. She stretched her wings and yawned. "Maybe we should do it tomorrow. I'm too tired."

Bellerophon sighed, his gaze on the stars. "Tomorrow night the stars will not be as bright," he said. "But I can wait."

Sam was even more tired than Joe or Polly. But he also wanted to fly again. "I think we should go tonight," he said. "It might be cloudy tomorrow."

Polly and Joe looked at each other. They had a feeling that Sam was right.

"Okay," said Joe.

"We'll fly by night," said Polly. "It's the last step from our paper."

"Uh-huh," Joe agreed. He was too tired to

be excited. "Let's at least have a little something to eat before we go."

With the blind man's help, they unstrapped the wings and took off the turtle-shell helmets. Then they ate the food Daedalus had given them and gulped water from their bottles. The snack gave them the strength to spread out the net.

"I hope it's strong enough," said Joe.

"It looks like magic to me," said Polly. "That should help."

Clio found extra leather straps in the backpack. Bellerophon used them to make loops at the net's corners. They pulled the net to the edge of the cliff beside the temple.

"Why is it always a cliff?" grumbled Polly. "I'd love to jump off a nice little hill."

Joe worried about the weight and whether they'd be able to fly or not.

Sam brought up another worry. "Didn't Bellerophon get in trouble for flying too high?"

"He was trying to get into the gods' home," said Polly. "This is different. I hope."

Bellerophon helped them put the wings back on. Then, holding on to Polly's feather, he lay in the center of the net, which he could see with the feather-sight.

Polly and Sam each held a long leather loop that went to a back corner of the net. Joe held a loop in each hand, one leading to one front corner, one leading to the other.

"We'd better have the wind's help," said Polly, crossing her fingers.

"I hope this works," said Joe.

Clio hooted, and they could feel the wind growing around them. It grew so strong that they didn't even need to jump off the cliff. The wind lifted them all together and pushed them into the sky.

Magically, Bellerophon and the net weighed nearly nothing. Higher and higher they rose, into the sparkling stars. The kids could faintly see the outlines of people and creatures in them, as if the power of Pegasus' feather could travel through the net to them.

They flew through thin layers of clouds.

The clouds were damp but not thick. The wind blew steadily.

Sam looked down at the old hero, who was sitting cross-legged in the golden net. Bellerophon's gaze was fixed on the stars. The feather rested in his lap.

"Pegasus!" cried Bellerophon, waving the feather.

The dim white horse in the sky lifted its heavy head and grew brighter. Then it saw Bellerophon. It gave a mighty neigh and climbed to its feet on the misty Milky Way. Then the white wings glowed as Pegasus spread them wide and leapt into the sky.

Sam, Polly, and Joe watched in wonder as the mythical creature soared toward them. Pegasus reached them and swooped around in majestic circles.

"Let me go," called Bellerophon. "Pegasus will catch me."

Pegasus neighed. Then the light weight of the net was gone. Pegasus had risen up below it. The three kids quickly let go of the leather straps and moved out of the way of the giant wings.

Sam, Polly, and Joe looked up. The sky had become crowded with other constellations watching. They could see them clearly, even without the help of the feather.

Bellerophon was seated on the winged horse's back, the fine net draped like a decorative saddle down Pegasus' sides. Together, they were much larger than life. Bellerophon had his arms around the horse's neck in a hug. When he sat back up, he was younger, with dark hair and a flashing smile and bright, clear eyes.

Bellerophon waved to the three kids as Pegasus climbed into the starry theater above, where all the people and creatures were cheering silently. Then all the figures slowly faded.

Sam, Polly, and Joe were alone in the starry sky.

CHAPTER TWELVE

Dream Feathers

Without the live constellations, the sky felt empty and the stars felt far away.

"Where's Clio?" asked Sam in a small voice.

"I don't see her," said Joe.

"Where do we go now?" said Polly. She was so tired she just wanted to sleep.

"Let's just go back to the temple," said Joe. "It should be right below us."

They made their way back down, spiraling and soaring lazily.

Then the ground that had been far away was close.

They all stumbled on their landings, but no one was hurt. They were in a field, and the temple was nowhere in sight.

"I guess we miscalculated," said Joe. He didn't even stand up from where he'd fallen.

"Hmmm," said Sam, and folded his wings as much as he could.

"We should get up," Polly murmured.

"Just a little rest," said Joe.

They woke to a gentle rocking. One by one, they opened their eyes. They were in Athena's chariot, flying in the place between times.

"I'm sorry I didn't see the reunion," said Athena, adjusting a new pair of sunglasses against the sun's glare. "I had something else to do, but Clio said it was wonderful."

"Um, thanks," said Joe blearily.

It took a moment for Polly to realize what the goddess was talking about. "Oh," she said. "Good."

Sam didn't even try to figure it out. He just rested his head on Polly's shoulder and fell back to sleep.

"We're there," said Athena as the chariot slid to the ground. "It's, oh, late afternoon or so."

The three kids groggily climbed out. They held on to the chariot so they could see it.

"I'm just dropping you off," said the goddess. "I'm very busy. Thank you for all your help. And thank your parents, too."

They nodded, then watched as the silver truck drove away.

Suddenly, it stopped in a cloud of dust. It backed up until it was in front of them again.

Athena leaned out toward them. "Come here."

They rested their hands on the edge of the door. The change back into the brightly colored world was startling again.

"Clio wanted you to have these," said Athena, handing each of them a small white feather. "They're hers."

Clio hooted.

"Oh, yes," said Athena, looking over her sunglasses. "In case you didn't know, these are dream feathers. Put them under your pillow or hold on to them while you sleep, and you'll dream of flying." The goddess smiled. "Very appropriate payment." Then she pushed her glasses up, and the silver truck pulled away again.

"Thanks," said Sam to the cloud of dust.

They turned and walked stiffly back to the campsite.

When they got there, they saw that the tents had been put away and the bags stacked up.

"How was it?" asked their father.

"Great," said Sam.

Polly nodded. "Yeah, it was."

"And very educational," said Joe, knowing that would make Dad happy.

"Did you see the bird?" asked their mother. "And where's Ann?"

"Oh, yeah, we found it," said Sam.

“She had to go back,” said Polly.

Their mother was looking at them intently. “You guys all look as if you’ve had a little too much sun.” She rummaged around in one of the bags and brought out bottles of water. “Drink,” she ordered. “Where’s your backpack?” she asked Joe as they gulped the water.

“Oh,” said Joe. “Uh, I think I forgot it in…um…maybe in Ath-Ann’s truck?”

Their mother sighed. “Another backpack gone.”

Dad cleared his throat. “Ahem,” he said. “We have some bad news.”

Joe choked on his water.

“It’s not *that* bad,” said Dad, thumping Joe on the back.

“It’s just, well, we’ve had enough camping,” Mom said apologetically.

“That’s okay,” said Sam.

“It is?” Both parents were surprised.

“Yeah,” said Polly.

“Mm-huh,” said Joe. “Let’s get this stuff packed up.” The thought of a warm, cozy, soft bed was almost more than he could stand.

Mom and Dad looked at each other and shrugged as their kids grabbed their bags and made for the car. "You just never know," said Mom.

As the car pulled onto the road, a soft west wind touched the windows. It looked in on three sleeping humans—each one holding a small white feather.

Don't miss the *next* book in

The Magic Elements Quartet

when Polly and Sam find

another message

and another mystery in

Fire Dreams.

Do you want to know more

about Greek myths?

Read

D'Aulaires' Book of Greek Myths

and

The Random House Book of Greek Myths

MALLORY LOEHR lives in Brooklyn, New York, and doesn't go camping very often. When she was growing up, one of the only camping trips she took with her parents was in an apple orchard in upstate New York. As she remembers, it rained the whole time. Some of her favorite authors growing up were (and still are!) Diana Wynne Jones, Lloyd Alexander, and Edward Eager. Ms. Loehr loves to read, write, play the piano, and dance the tango. Athena is her favorite of the Greek gods and goddesses. Hermes and Artemis run close seconds.